This igloo book belongs to:

Published in 2020
by Igloo Books Ltd
Cottage Farm
Sywell
NN6 0BJ
www.igloobooks.com

Copyright © 2014 Igloo Books Ltd
Igloo Books is an imprint of Bonnier Books UK

0620 002
2 4 6 8 10 9 7 5 3
ISBN 978-1-78905-679-2

Written by Melanie Joyce
Illustrated by James Newman Gray

Printed and manufactured in China

# Through the Starlight Window

igloobooks

"Look through the starlight window,"
said Dad to Little Bear.
"Everyone is settling down
and going to sleep out there."

dow's edge, comes a tired field mouse,

rriedly back home to his cosy house.

By the brook, the little fawn
nods his sleepy head.
"Come on, little one," says Mum.
"It's time you were in bed."

In their burrows, fluffy
bunnies cuddle in moonbeams.
Daddy bunny kisses them,
as they settle down to dream.

From the quiet beehive comes the hum of sleepy bees,
as moles dive in their holes, deep down, beneath the trees.

On the shimmering pond, fluffy ducklings still their wings,
as ripples of bright water float away in little rings.

In the moonlit stable,
a foal nuzzles his mummy.
She gently strokes his head
and he snuggles to her tummy.

Along the garden path, the hedgehogs quietly creep,
snuffling in the shadows as they go back home to sleep.

Through the starlight window,
one tired teddy bear
cuddles up in Daddy's arms
and dreams without a care.

Now Little Bear is fast asleep
and snoozing by starlight.
Daddy Bear kisses him gently
and softly says, "Goodnight."